MALCOLM'S MARTIANS: EXPLORING MARS

The Rising Tide of Lava: Chaos on Mars

by Jason M. Burns

illustrated by Dustin Evans

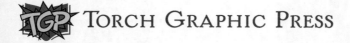

TORCH GRAPHIC PRESS

Published in the United States of America by Cherry Lake Publishing Group
Ann Arbor, Michigan
www.cherrylakepublishing.com

Reading Adviser: Beth Walker Gambro, MS, Ed., Reading Consultant, Yorkville, IL

Book Designer: Book Buddy Media

Torch Graphic Press is an imprint of Cherry Lake Publishing Group.

Library of Congress Cataloging-in-Publication Data has been filed and is available at catalog.loc.gov

Cherry Lake Publishing Group would like to acknowledge the work of the Partnership for 21st Century
Learning, a Network of Battelle for Kids. Please visit http://www.battelleforkids.org/networks/p21 for
more information.

Printed in the United States of America
Corporate Graphics

TABLE OF CONTENTS

Mission log: August 26, 2055.

I once went on a trip to the Grand Canyon. It was so amazing. I couldn't believe something that big could exist. Well, Dad told me this morning that we are going to visit the Valles Marineris. It's a huge valley on Mars that could swallow the Grand Canyon whole. My friend, Daniela, was so excited she squeaked like a Martian. At least, that's how I imagine Martians sound. We will see what kind of Martians we run into at the Valles Marineris!

—Malcolm Thomas

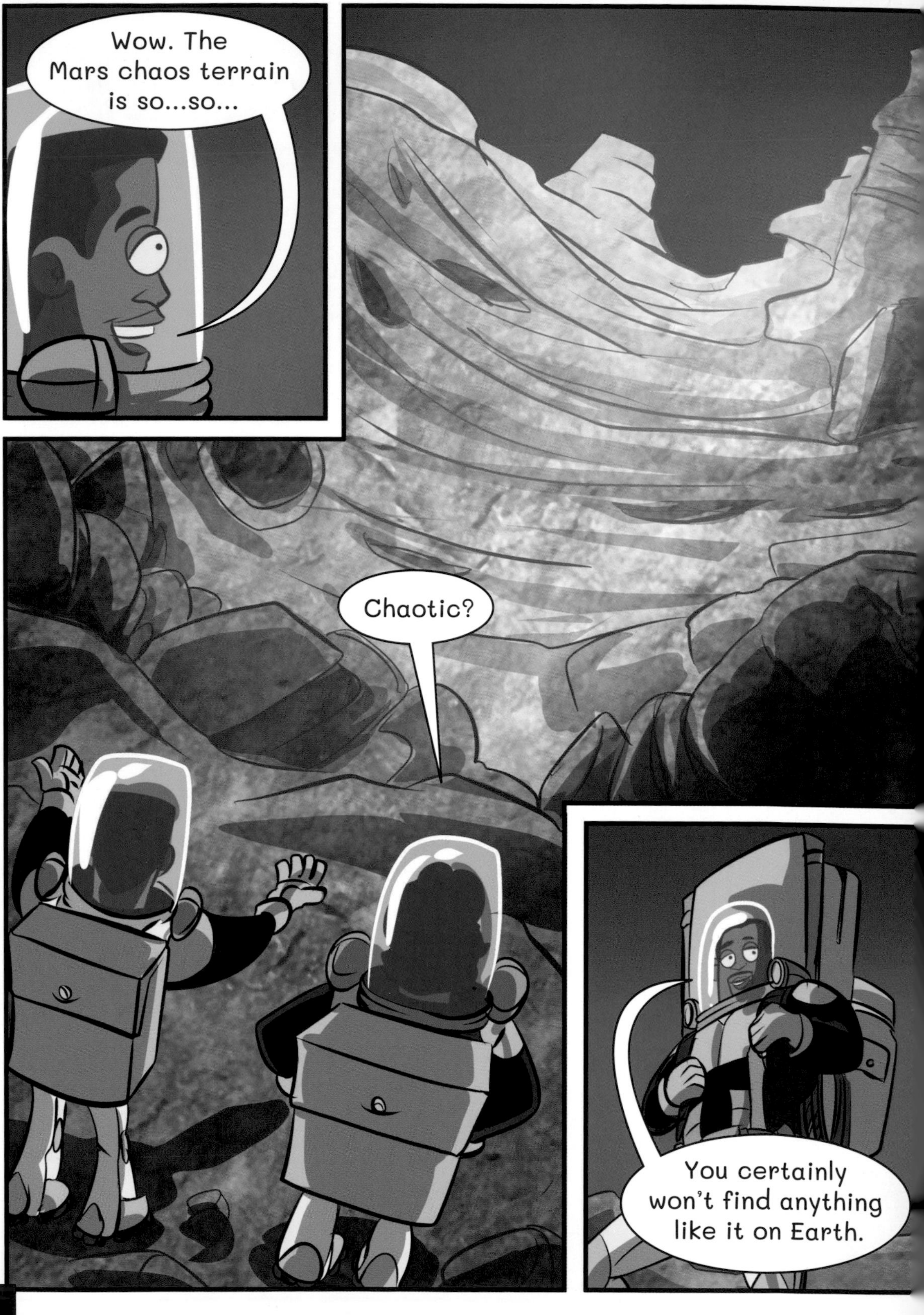

Wow. The Mars chaos terrain is so...so...
Chaotic?
You certainly won't find anything like it on Earth.

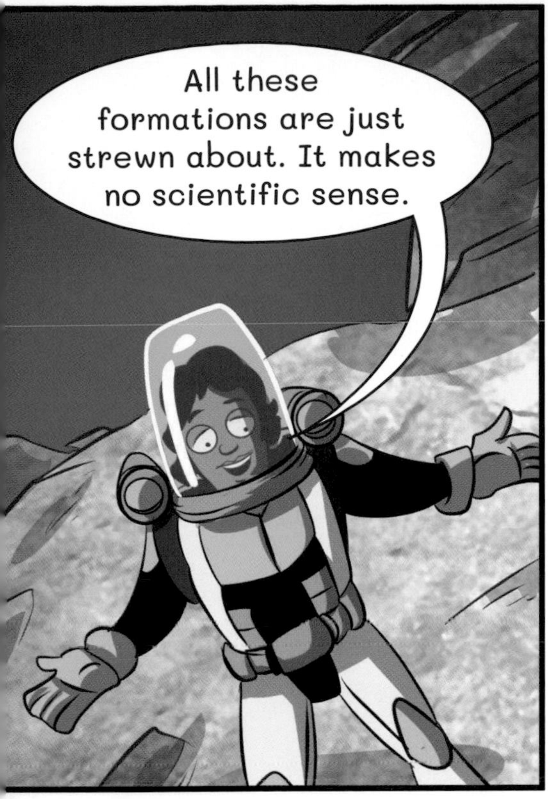
All these formations are just strewn about. It makes no scientific sense.

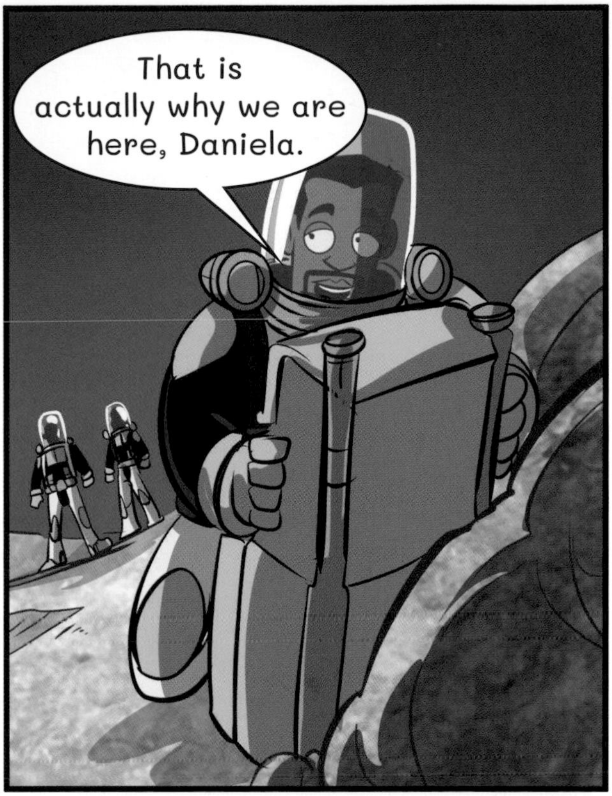
That is actually why we are here, Daniela.

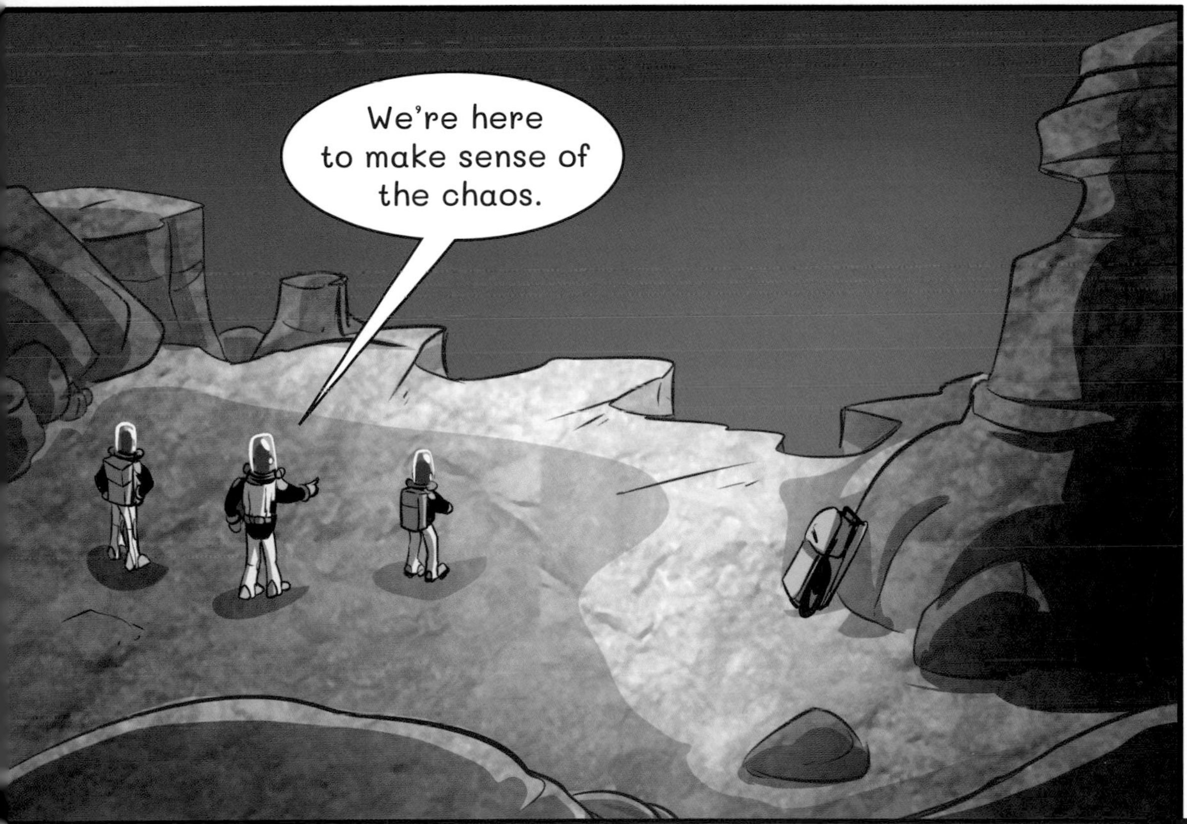
We're here to make sense of the chaos.

So this is the Mars version of the Grand Canyon.

It's grander than the Grand Canyon. The Valles Marineris is 5 times as long and 4 times as deep.

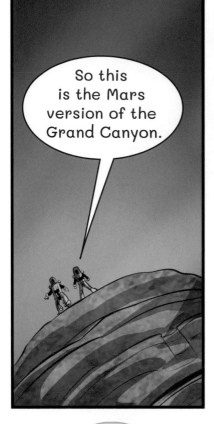

MARS FACT

Portions of the Valles Marineris are believed to be 4 miles (7 kilometers) deep. The Grand Canyon's average depth is 1 mile (1.6 km).

What are all of these holes in the ground?

I'm picking up an increased heat signature coming from inside.

And I can hear gurgling.

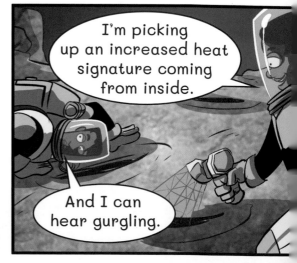

THE CASE FOR SPACE

There is a lot we don't know about the Mars chaos region. But there are also plenty of theories about how this unique landscape was formed. Let's dig into the Red Planet's past to understand a bit about what is going on in the present.

•Valles Marineris is part of the chaos terrain. The terrain is also littered with **mesas**, **buttes**, hills, canyons, and valleys.

•There is nothing like the chaos terrain on Earth. No similar discoveries have been made in the solar system, either.

•The various formations suggest that something—maybe water—altered the landscape quickly.

•There are theories that Mars was once covered by water. When the planet cooled, the water froze.

•The ice then melted quickly. Scientists think this was from **magma** rising up from under the planet's crust. It washed over the land. This produced all of the valleys and mesas that are visible on Mars's surface.

•Scientists have been able to study photographs of these structures. These photographs show even channels that look like the kind that are made when something overflows. This is additional evidence that water had a hand in their creation.

mesas: hills or mountains with a flat top
buttes: tall towers of rock with a flat surface
magma: liquid rock that is extremely hot

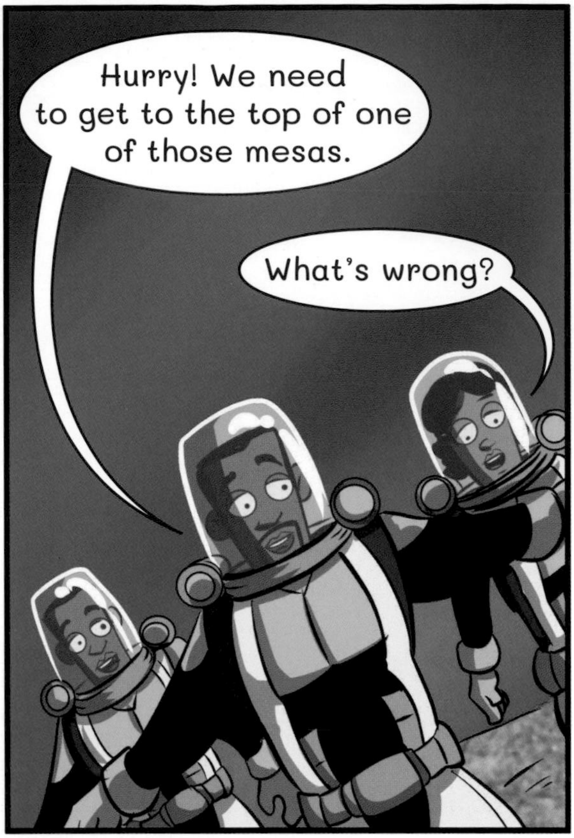
Hurry! We need to get to the top of one of those mesas.
What's wrong?

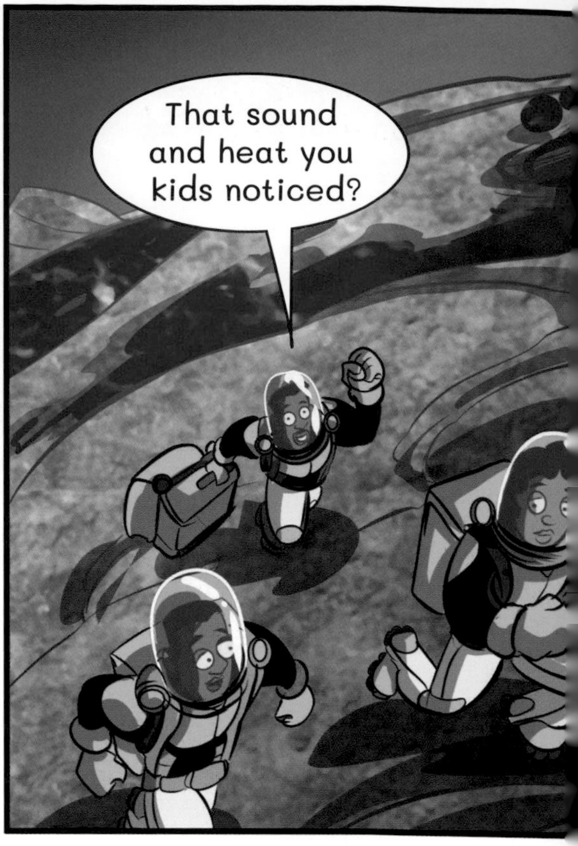
That sound and heat you kids noticed?

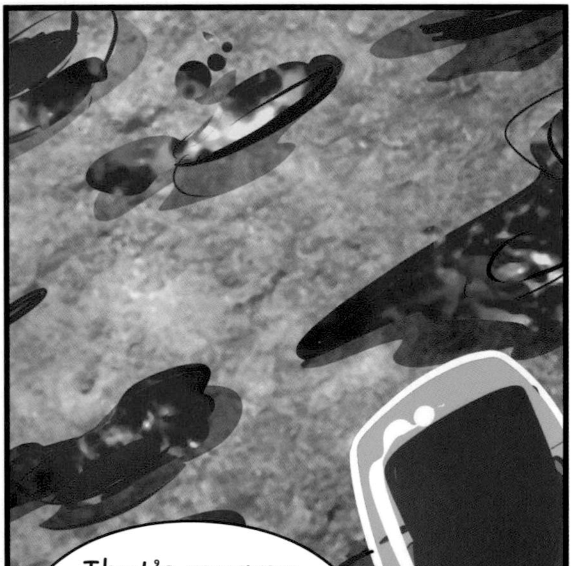
That's magma. And it's bubbling to the surface—right now!

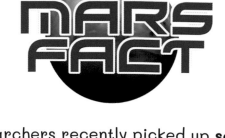

MARS FACT

Researchers recently picked up **sei** signals from a Mars volcano. They b this to be evidence of underground magma ready to come to the surfac

seismic: vibrations in the landscape, b above ground and below

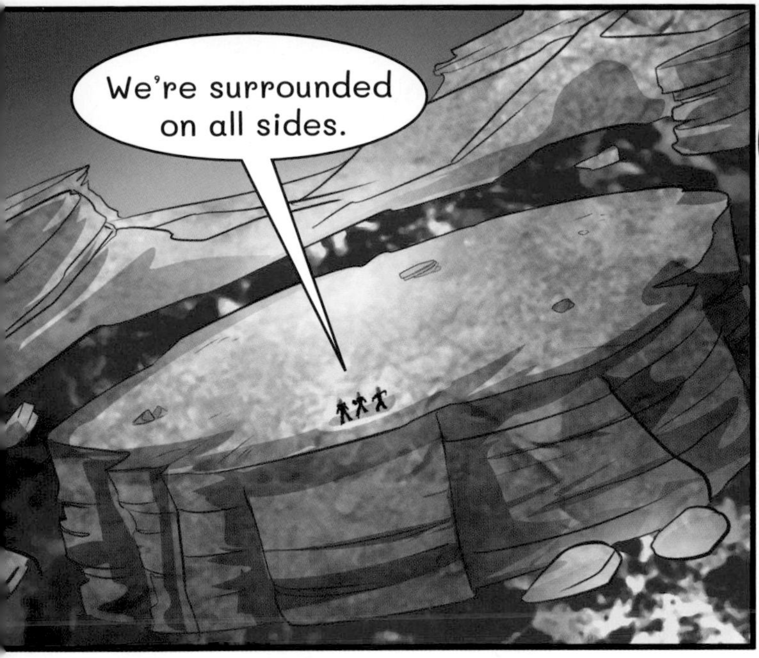
We're surrounded on all sides.

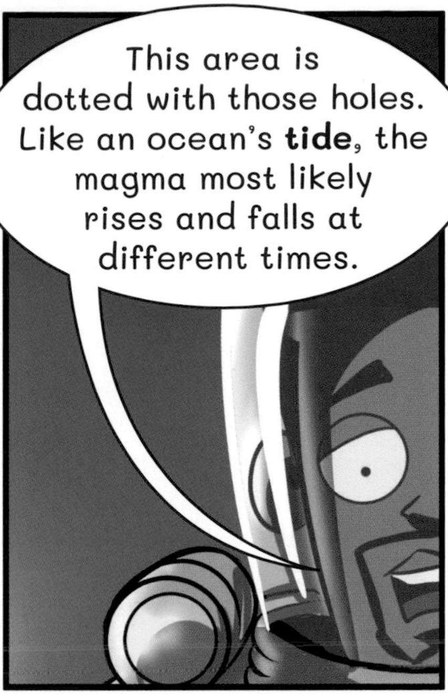
This area is dotted with those holes. Like an ocean's **tide**, the magma most likely rises and falls at different times.

SCIENCE FACT

Tides on Earth are caused by the Moon. The Moon has a **gravitational pull** that creates a tidal force. This force causes the water to bulge towards the Moon. This is why the oceans rise and fall.

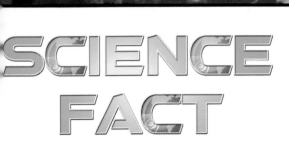

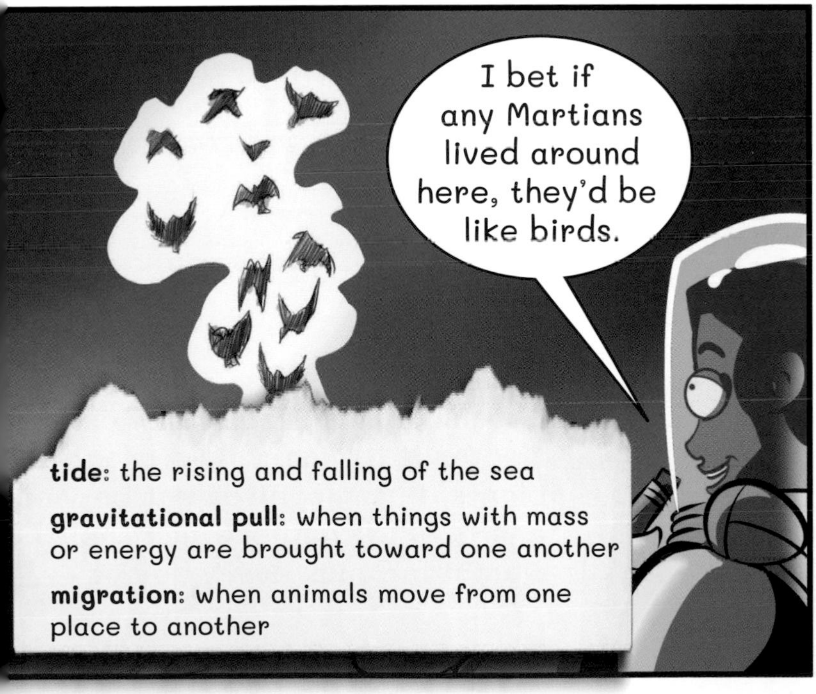
I bet if any Martians lived around here, they'd be like birds.

tide: the rising and falling of the sea

gravitational pull: when things with mass or energy are brought toward one another

migration: when animals move from one place to another

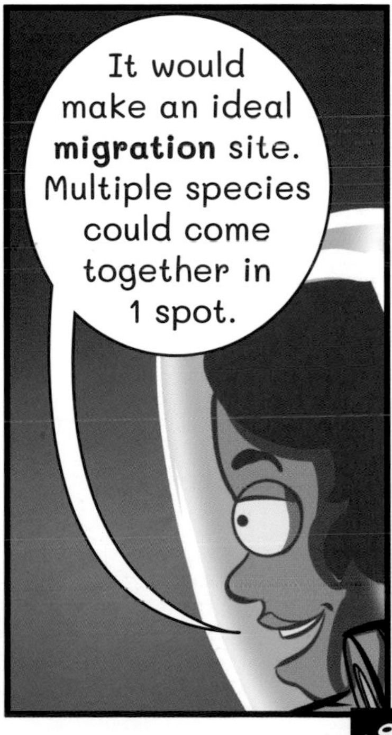
It would make an ideal **migration** site. Multiple species could come together in 1 spot.

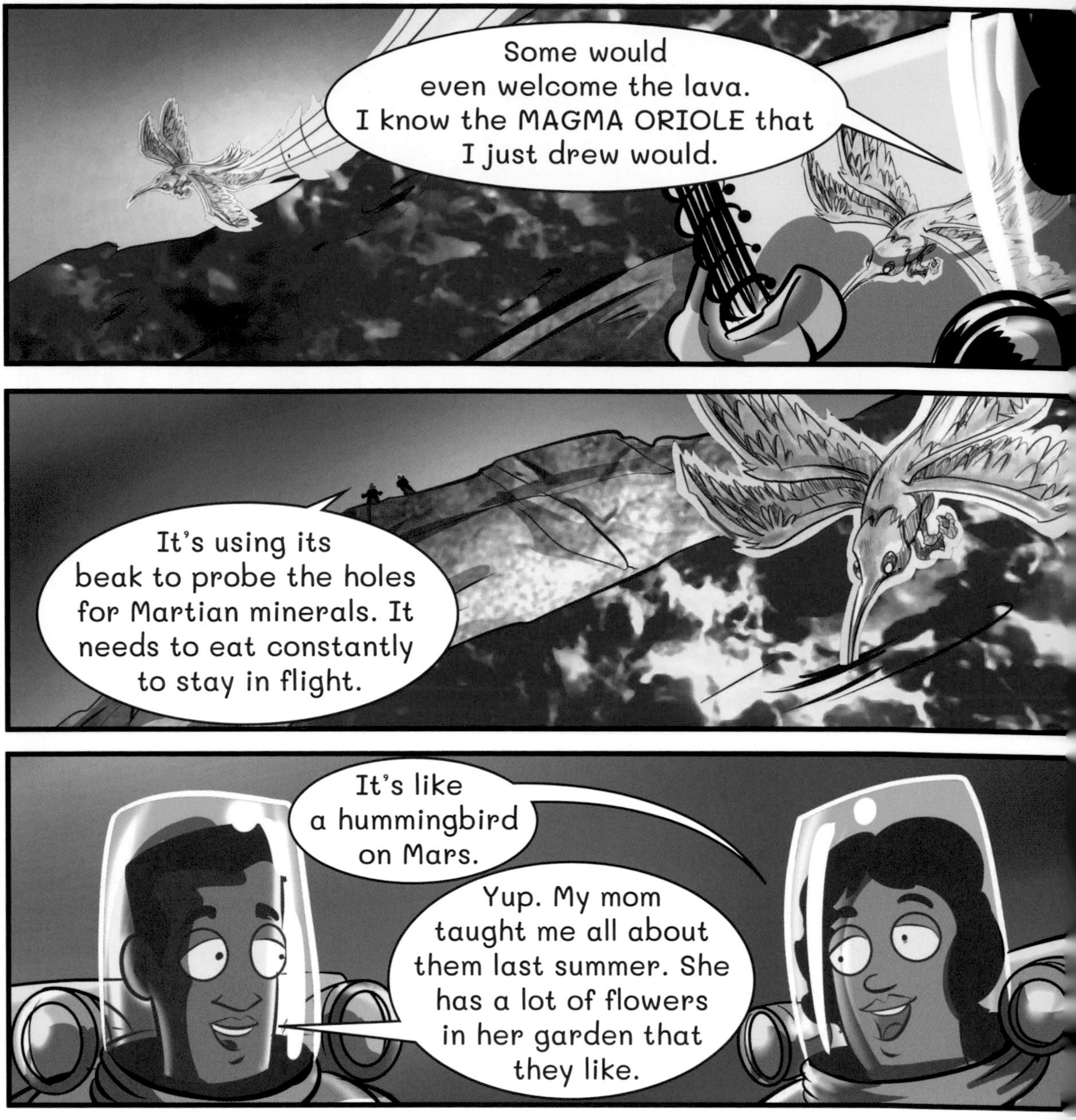
Some would even welcome the lava. I know the MAGMA ORIOLE that I just drew would.
It's using its beak to probe the holes for Martian minerals. It needs to eat constantly to stay in flight.
It's like a hummingbird on Mars.
Yup. My mom taught me all about them last summer. She has a lot of flowers in her garden that they like.

SCIENCE FACT

Hummingbirds feed mostly on nect
Nectar is a sugary fluid created b
plants. Hummingbirds eat betwee
one-quarter and one-half their bo
weight in sugar every day.

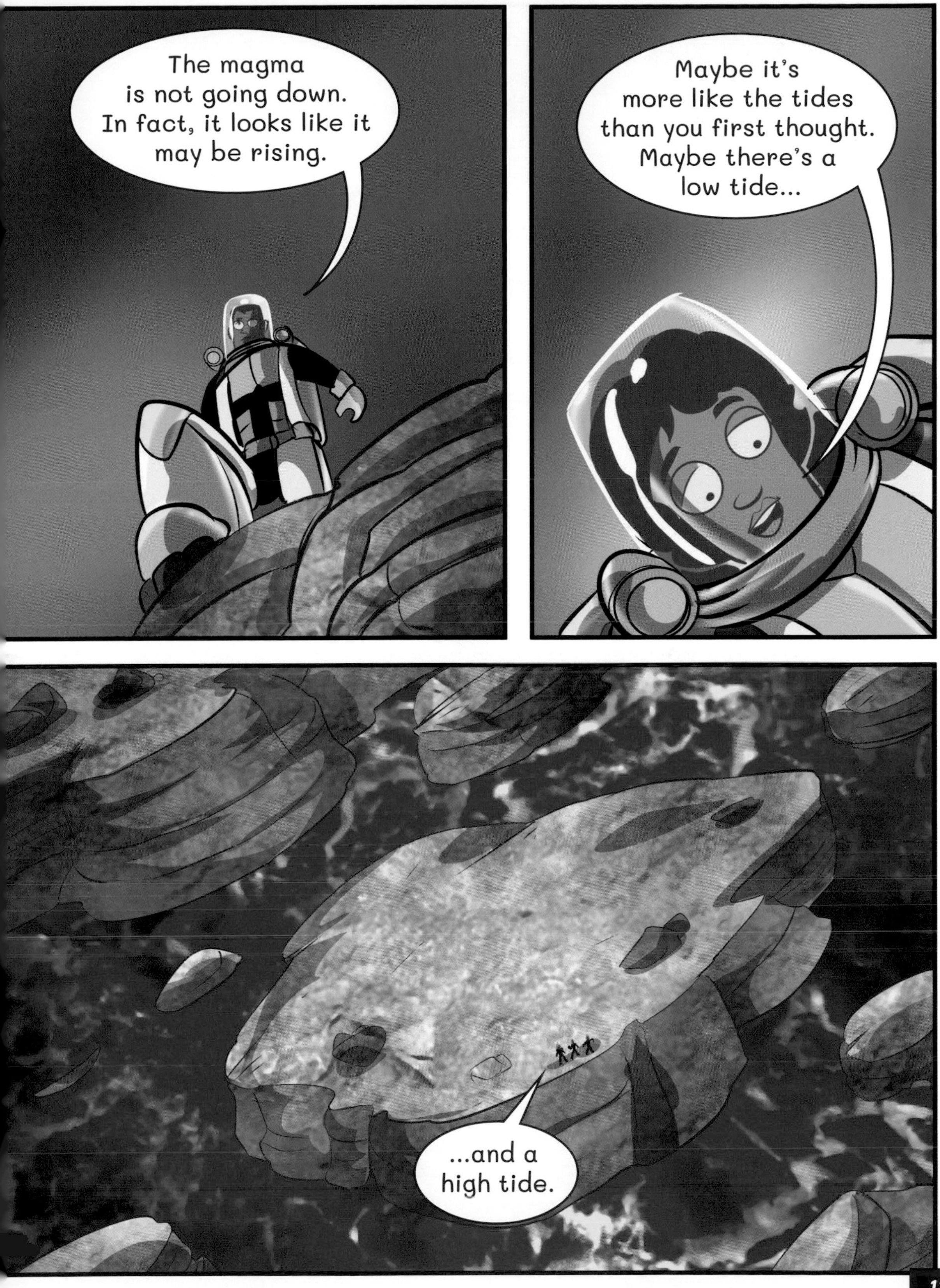
The magma is not going down. In fact, it looks like it may be rising.
Maybe it's more like the tides than you first thought. Maybe there's a low tide...
...and a high tide.

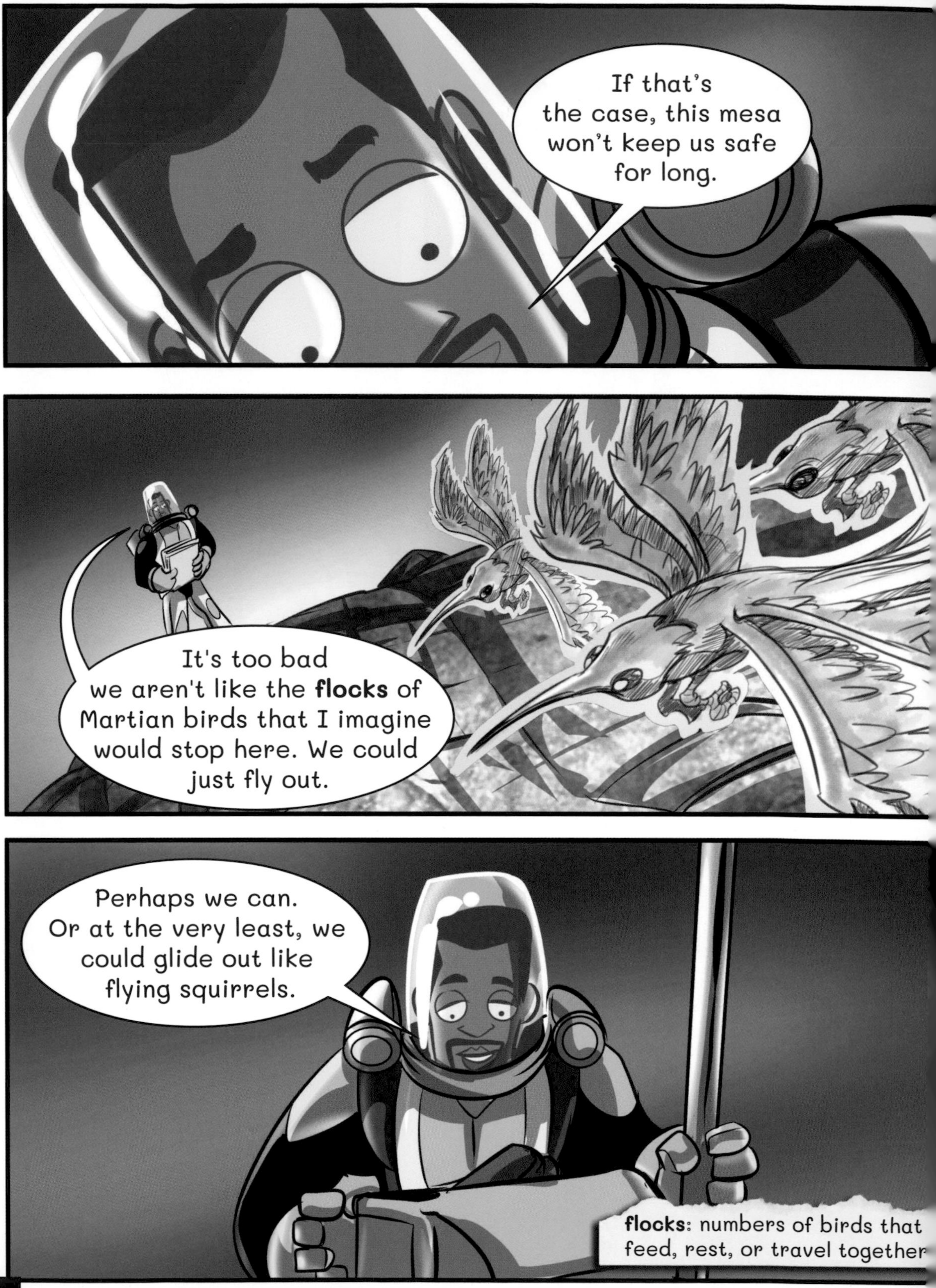
If that's the case, this mesa won't keep us safe for long.
It's too bad we aren't like the **flocks** of Martian birds that I imagine would stop here. We could just fly out.
Perhaps we can. Or at the very least, we could glide out like flying squirrels.

flocks: numbers of birds that feed, rest, or travel together

THE SCIENCE OF SCIENCE FICTION

Right now, it's just fun to imagine ourselves traveling into space. But is it really that unbelievable? In the near future, it won't be just astronauts flying off in a shuttle. Let's take a look at one of the most exciting subjects in space travel—tourism.

•Numerous companies have their sights set on space tourism, including Virgin Galactic, Blue Origin, and SpaceX.

•Space tourism is also called citizen space exploration.

•Most of these trips will be sub-orbital spaceflight. That means the spacecraft will fly up into space, and then fall back down. Orbital flight needs faster-moving spacecraft. The spacecraft will have to travel fast enough to stay in orbit around the planet.

•Space tourism will not be cheap. Sub-orbital flights will cost hundreds of thousands of dollars per person.

•Space travel is physically demanding. Not everyone will be able to make the trip.

•The first space tourist was Dennis Tito. In 2001, the wealthy businessman paid $20 million to travel to the International Space Station.

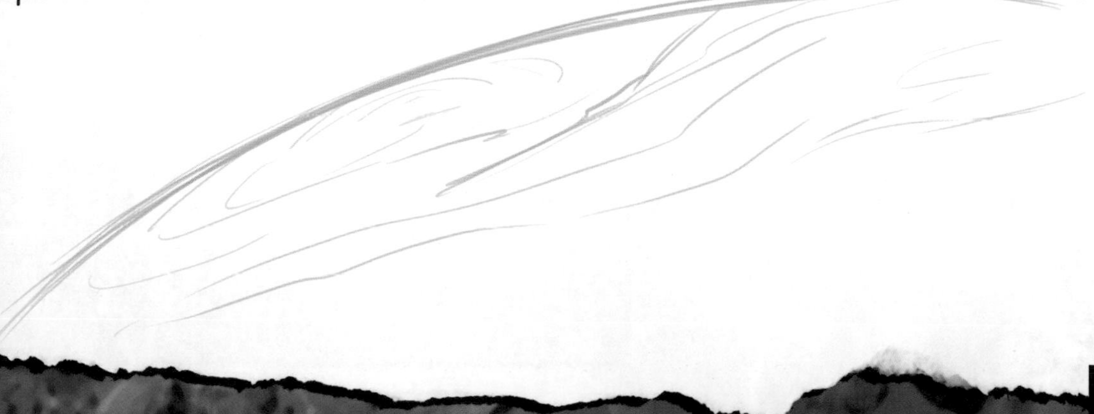

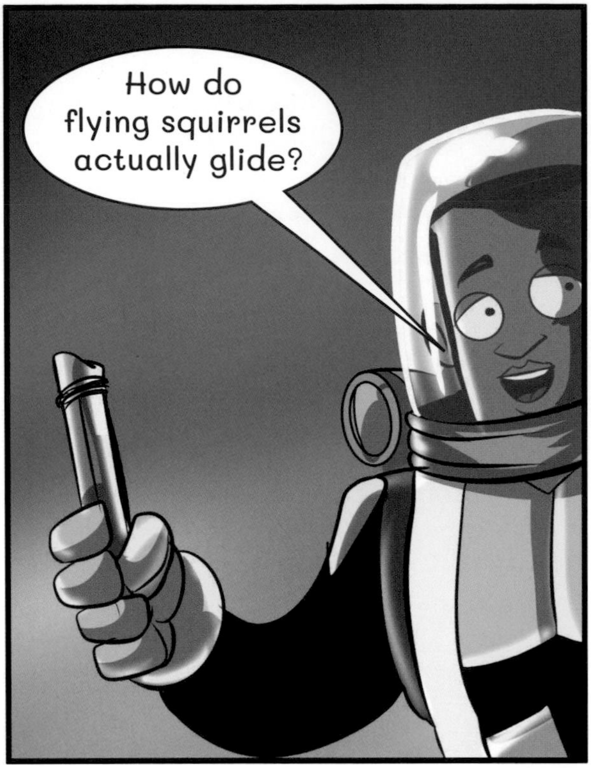
How do flying squirrels actually glide?

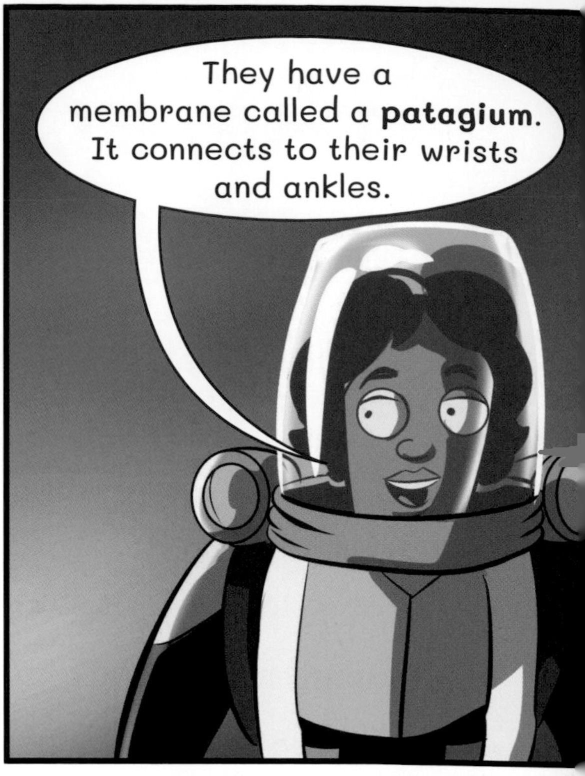
They have a membrane called a **patagium**. It connects to their wrists and ankles.

SCIENCE FACT

Flying dinosaurs called pterosaurs also had patagium.

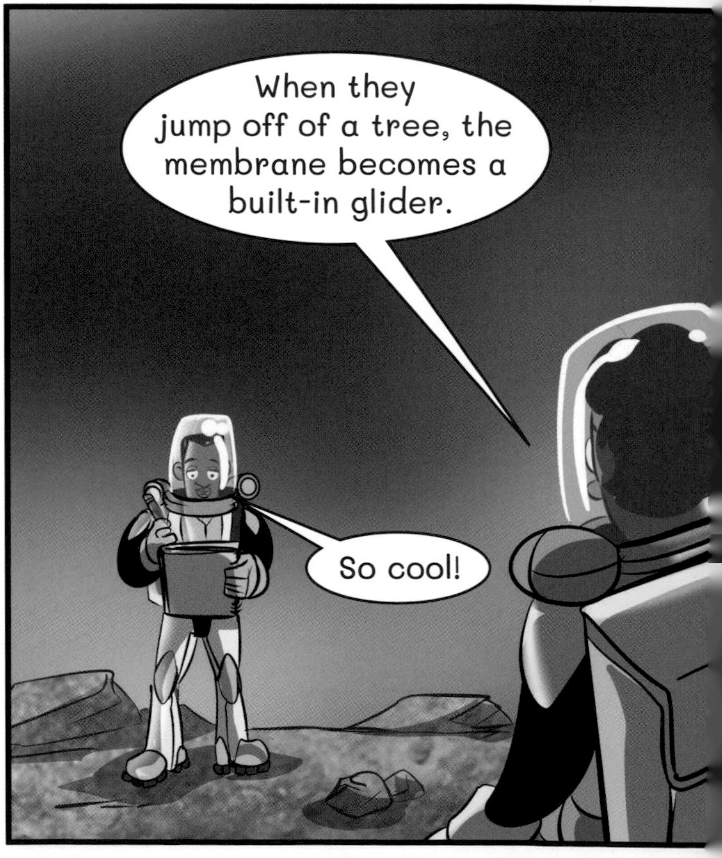
When they jump off of a tree, the membrane becomes a built-in glider.
So cool!

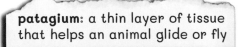

patagium: a thin layer of tissue that helps an animal glide or fly

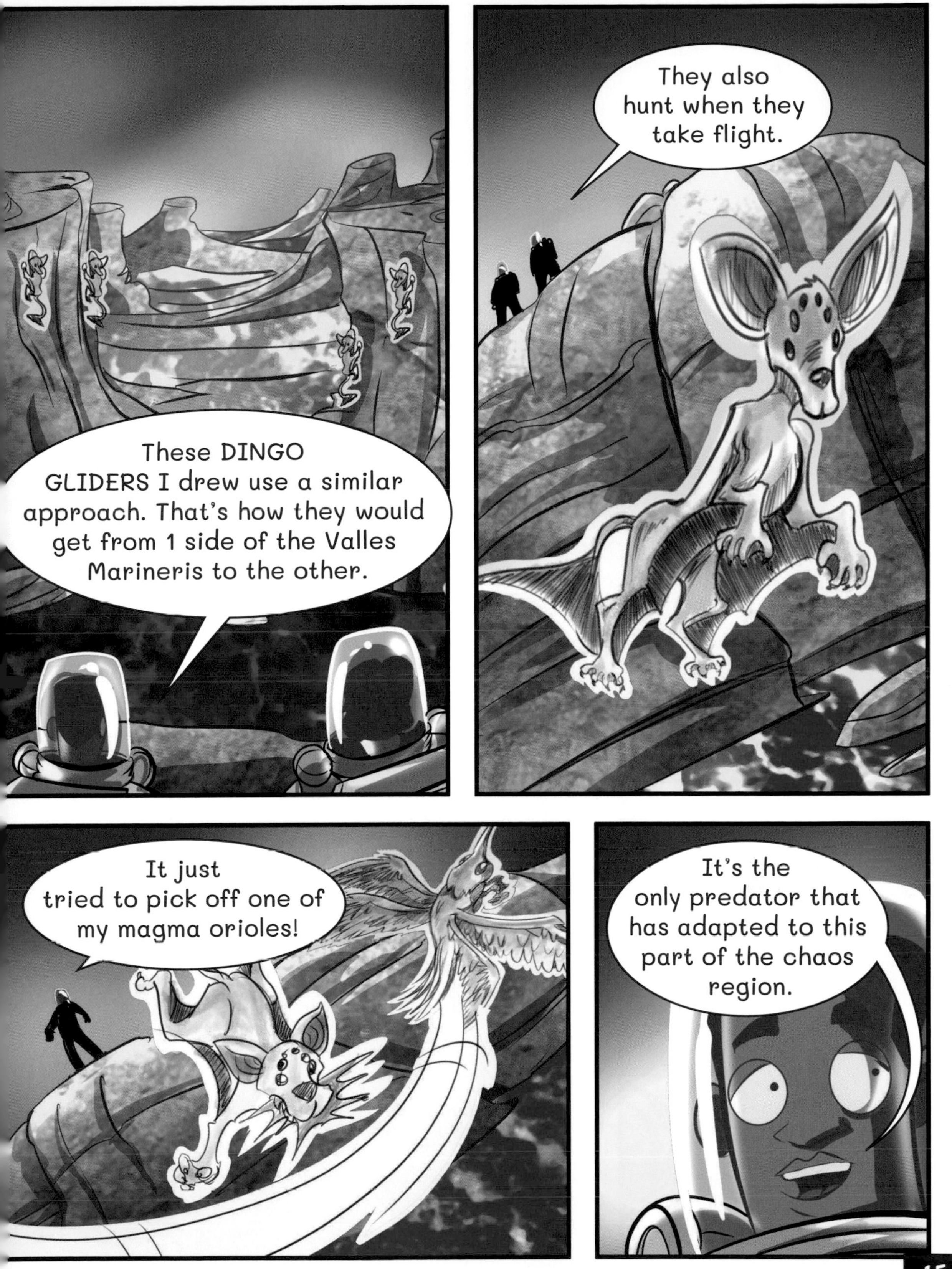
These DINGO GLIDERS I drew use a similar approach. That's how they would get from 1 side of the Valles Marineris to the other.
They also hunt when they take flight.
It just tried to pick off one of my magma orioles!
It's the only predator that has adapted to this part of the chaos region.

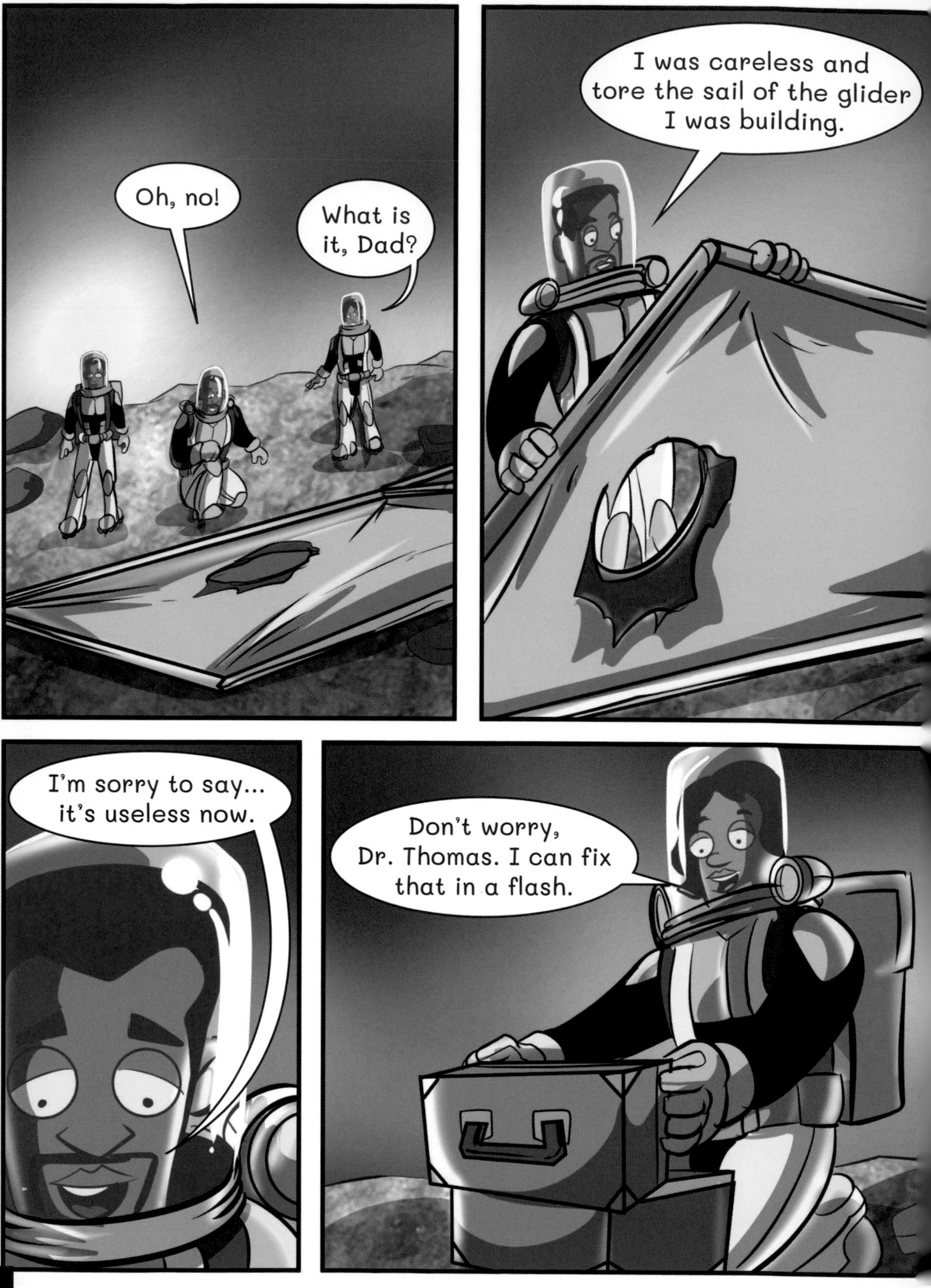
Oh, no!
What is it, Dad?
I was careless and tore the sail of the glider I was building.
I'm sorry to say... it's useless now.
Don't worry, Dr. Thomas. I can fix that in a flash.

Last year I won the local science fair by putting a new spin on an old classic.

I invented an extra strong **liquid latex** that is perfect for a situation like this.

See? It's like new!

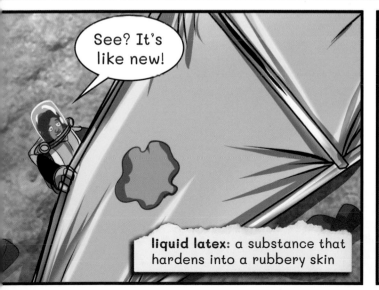

liquid latex: a substance that hardens into a rubbery skin

You kids never cease to amaze me.

We have another problem.

The magma tide seems to be coming in faster now.

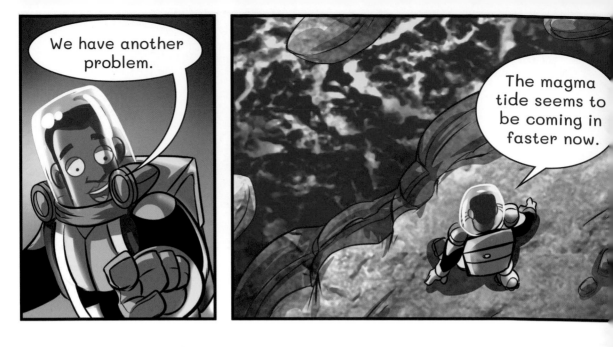

SCIENCE FACT

On Earth, there are 2 high tides a
2 low tides every day. The height difference between high tide and low tide is called tidal range.

We have to go. Now.
But can we even get the same lift on Mars, given its thinner atmosphere?

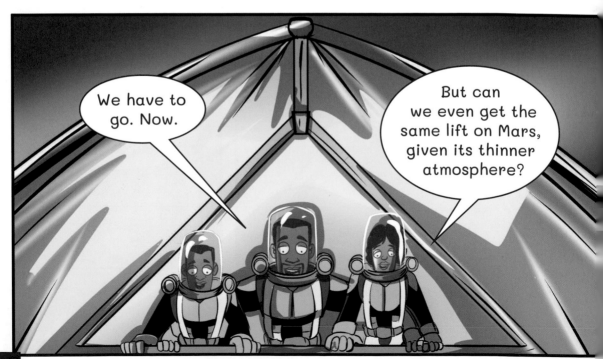

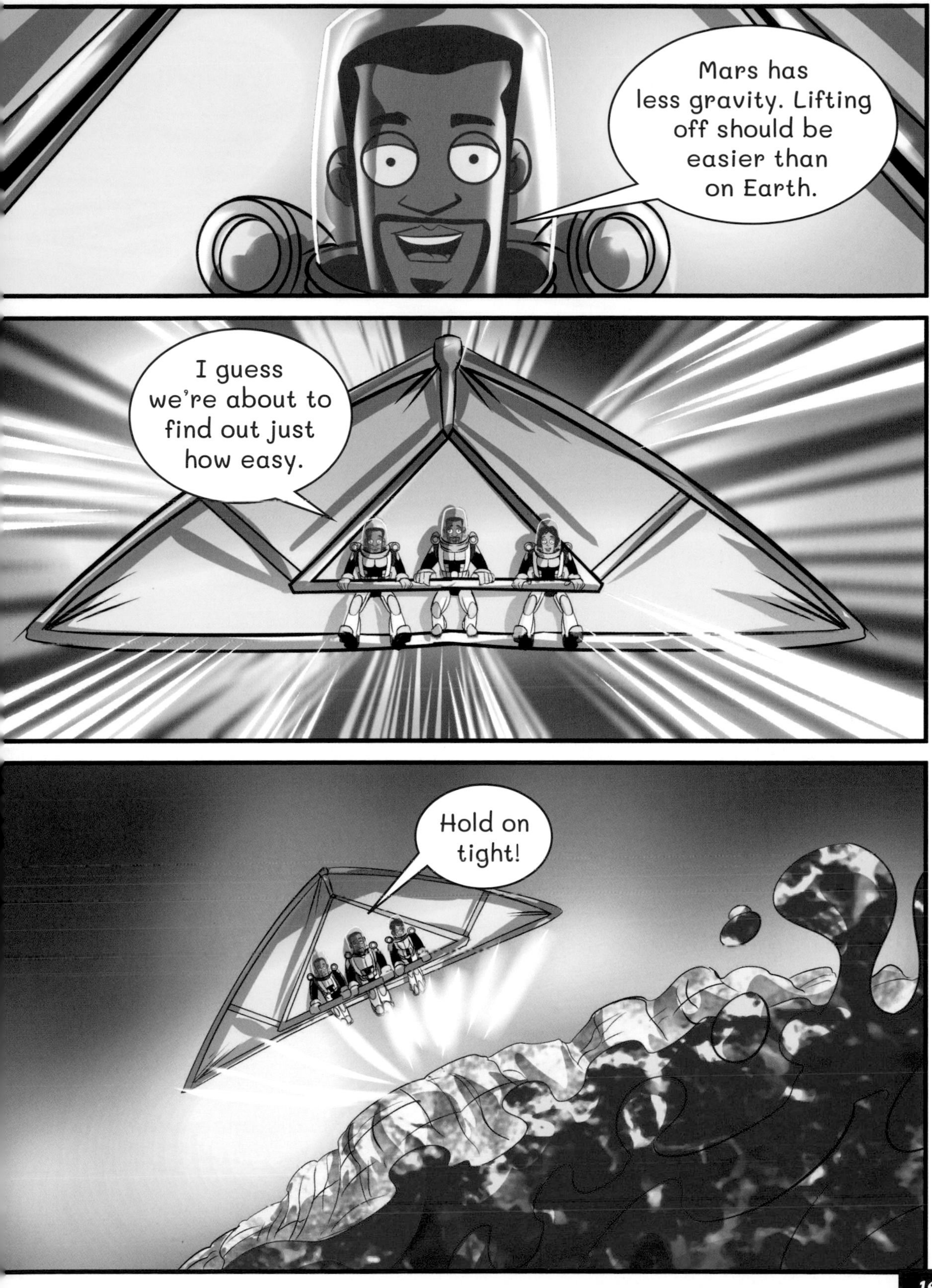
Mars has less gravity. Lifting off should be easier than on Earth.
I guess we're about to find out just how easy.
Hold on tight!

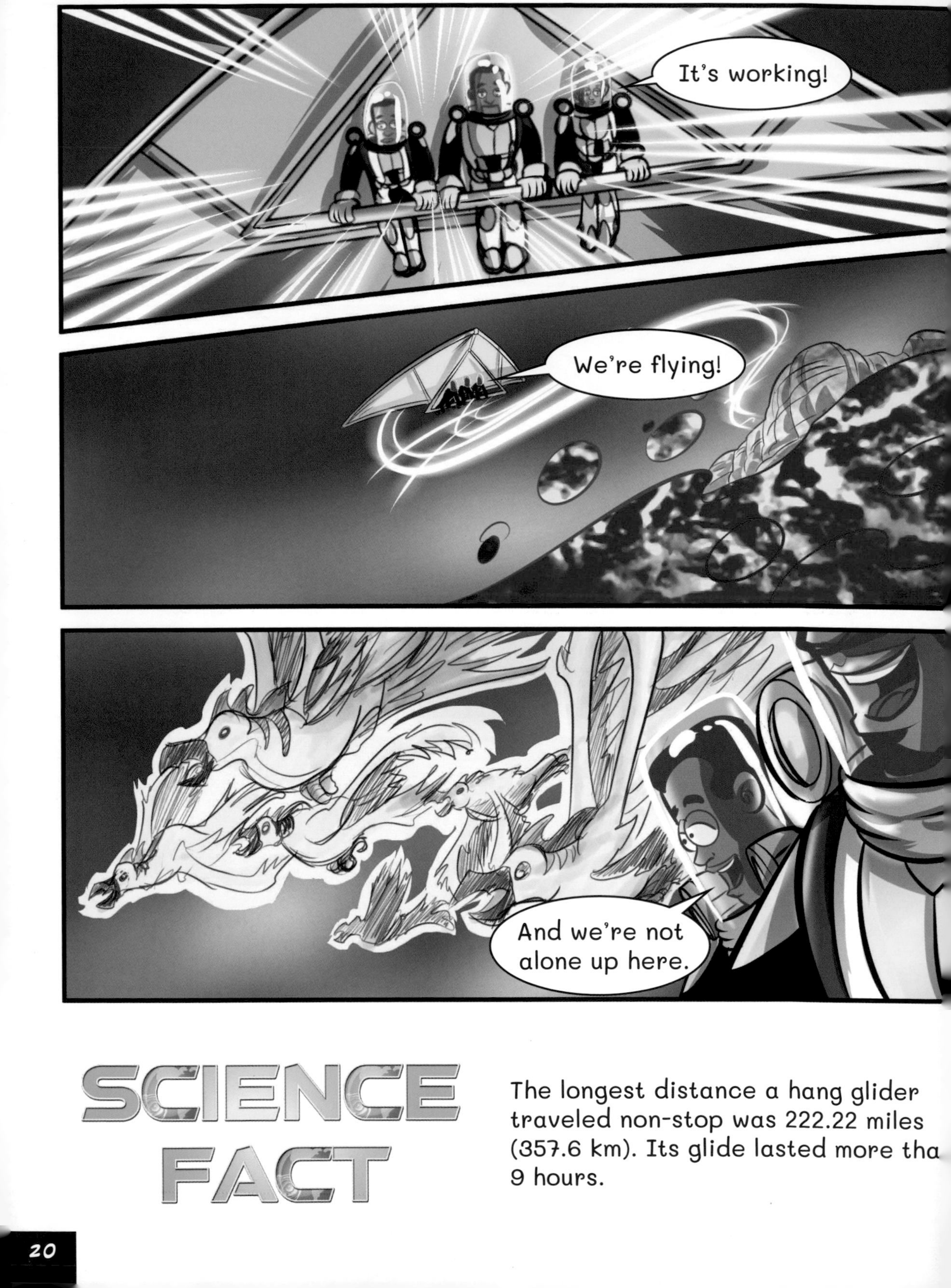
It's working!
We're flying!
And we're not alone up here.

SCIENCE FACT

The longest distance a hang glider traveled non-stop was 222.22 miles (357.6 km). Its glide lasted more tha 9 hours.

THE FUNDAMENTALS OF ART

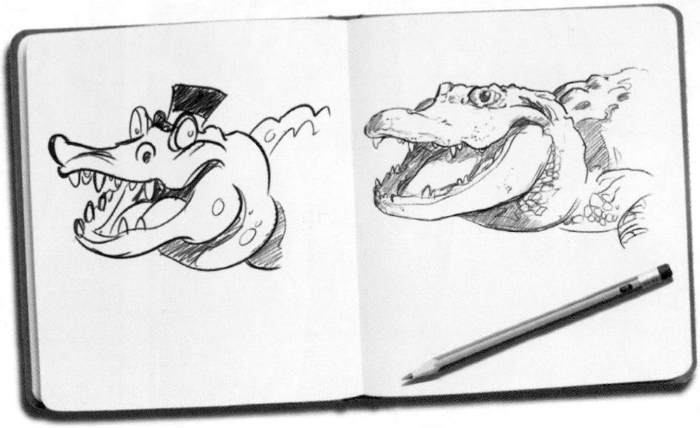

Let's put the FUN in the fundamentals of art by learning how to draw lifelike animals. Malcolm uses his imagination to create his Martians, but he couldn't do it without first having a strong understanding of the animal kingdom. So, what does it take to make a tiger look like a tiger? We're here to show you!

•Observe or watch videos on the animals you want to draw. Learn how the animal moves and acts.

•Study photographs. Discover the features that make a particular animal unique.

•Learn about basic anatomy. Understanding how things like joints work will make your drawings more lifelike.

•Start by drawing 1 part of the animal, like the head. Practice that area until you are comfortable and then move on to the next part. Breaking the animal down will make the task seem less daunting.

•Pay attention to proportions. You want the parts of the animal to work together just as they do in real life. A tiger with a head too big for its body will not look lifelike.

ARTIST TIP: One thing that can help bring your animal drawings to life is a pattern. Study photos of animals like lizards, zebras, giraffes, or even frogs. Notice the shapes that make up their stripes, spots, and scales. Then use them in your drawings.

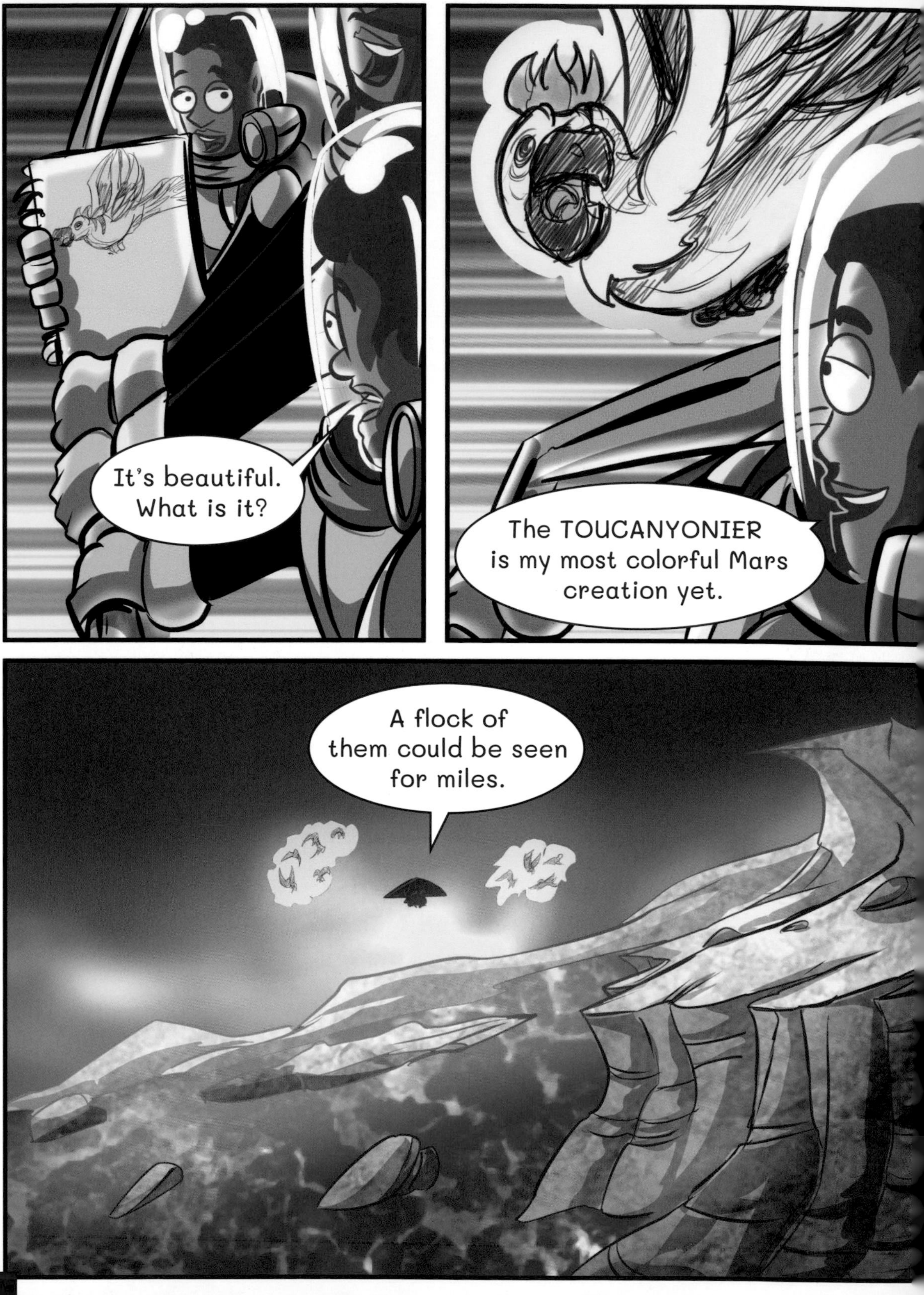
It's beautiful. What is it?
The TOUCANYONIER is my most colorful Mars creation yet.
A flock of them could be seen for miles.

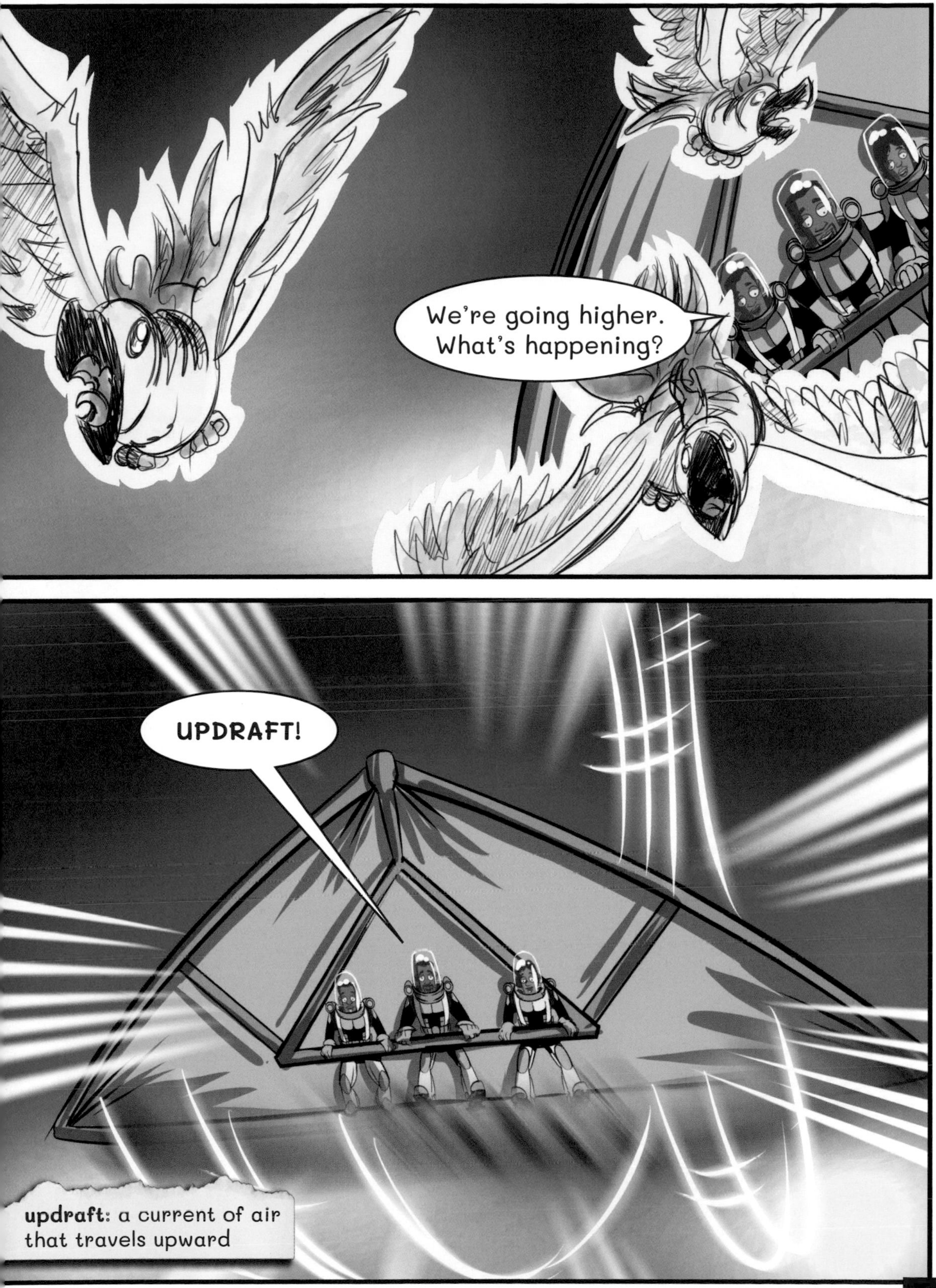
We're going higher. What's happening?
UPDRAFT!
updraft: a current of air that travels upward

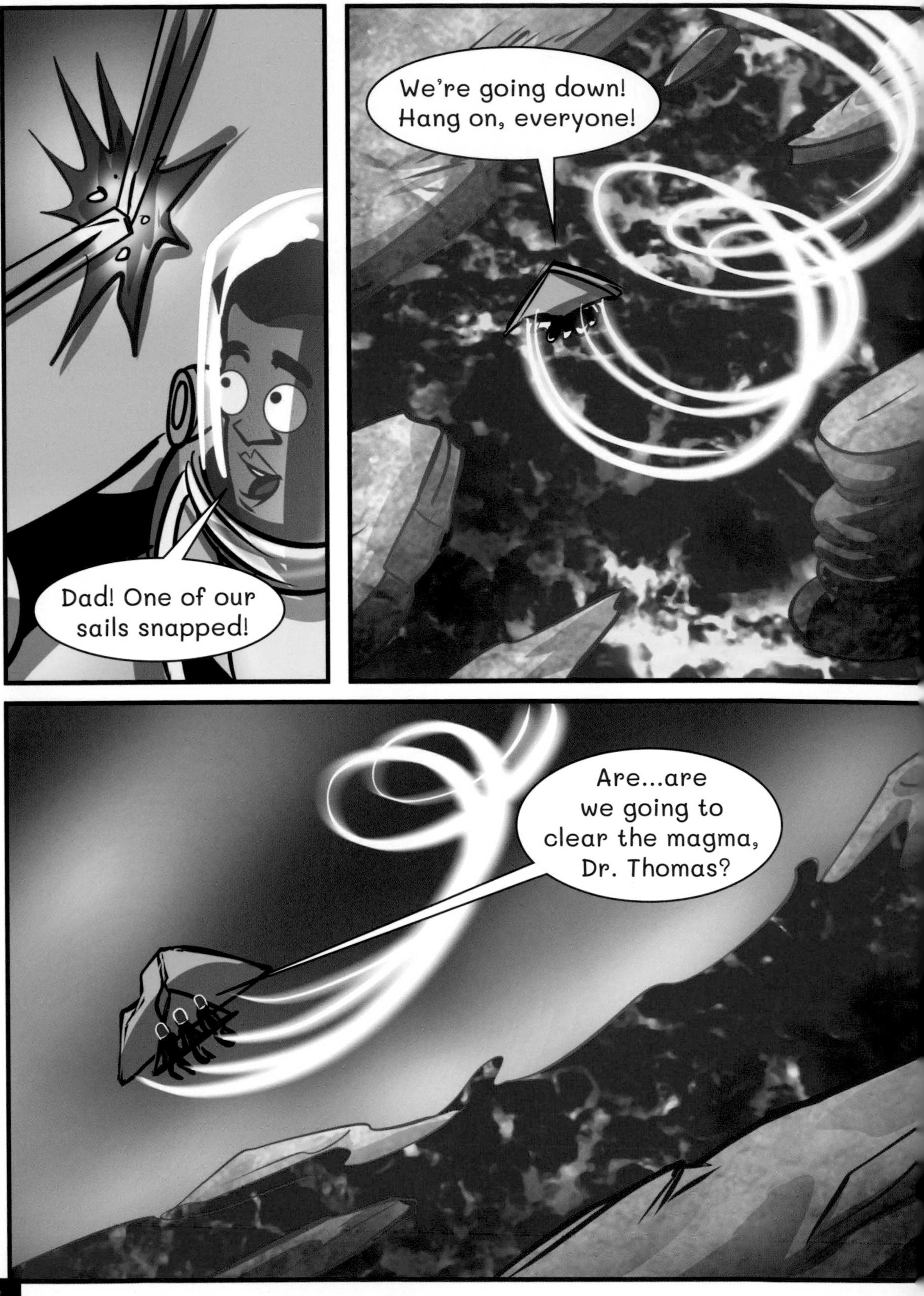
Dad! One of our sails snapped!
We're going down! Hang on, everyone!
Are...are we going to clear the magma, Dr. Thomas?

MARS SURVIVAL TIPS

Whether you are flying on Mars or on Earth, it's important to know what to do in case of an emergency. Stay calm and follow the tips below.

- Wear fitted clothing when flying. Baggy shirts and pants are more likely to get caught on things.

- Choose clothes made of cotton or other natural materials. In case there's a fire, these fabrics hold up better than synthetic ones.

- Listen to the preflight safety protocols. They are presented for a reason.

- Secure your seat belt. Practice undoing it a few times, so you know how it works.

- Put on the oxygen mask as soon as it appears.

- Brace for impact by leaning forward and pressing your head against the seat in front of you. This limits your chance of injury.

- Remain calm. Panicking will just place you in more danger.

- Fire spreads quickly after a crash. You may only have 1 to 2 minutes to escape. Know your exits and move.

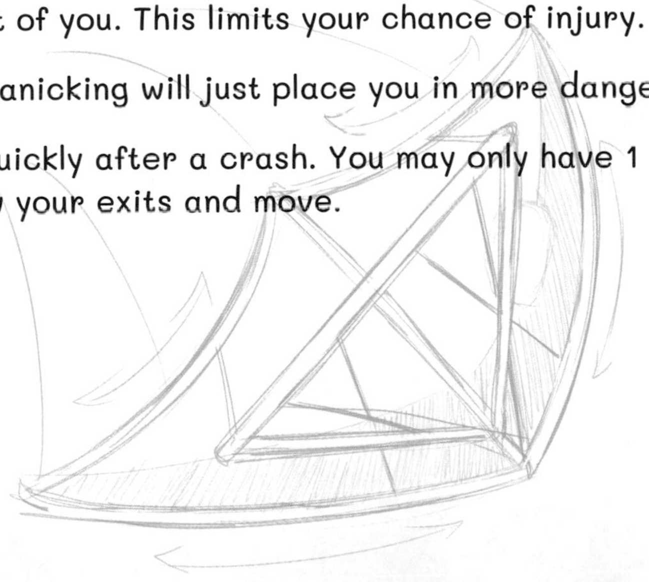

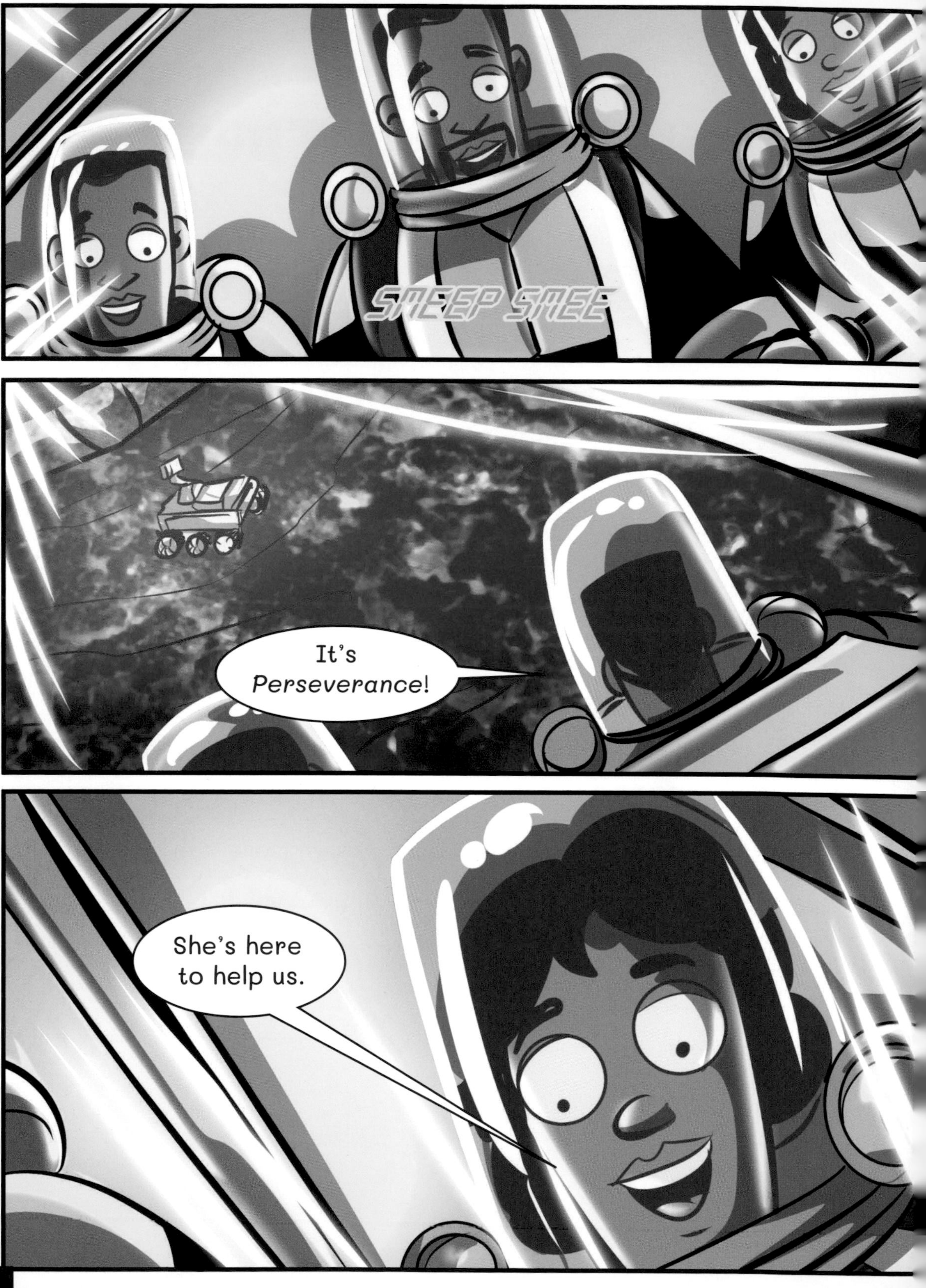
SWEEP SWEE
It's Perseverance!
She's here to help us.

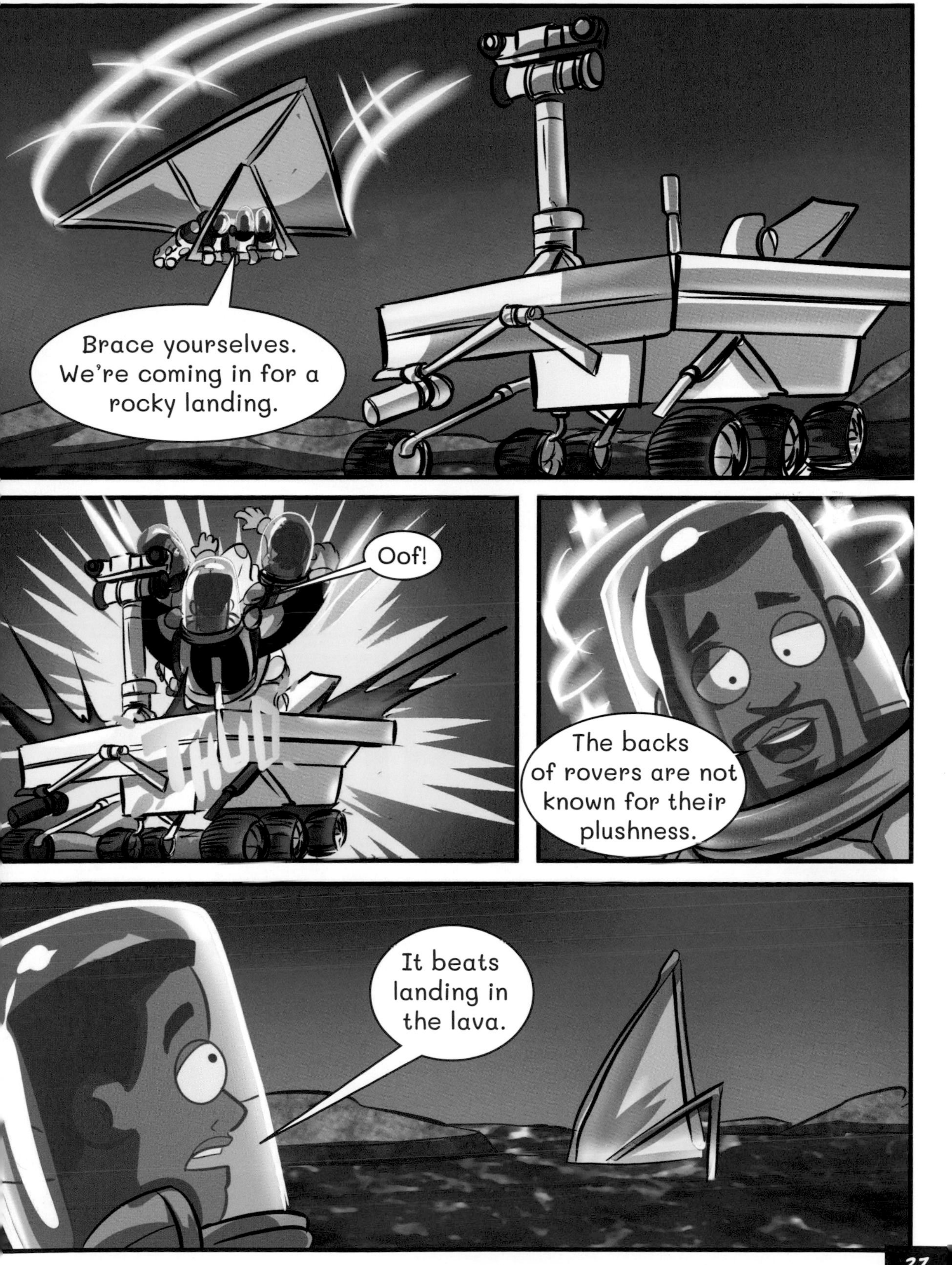
Brace yourselves. We're coming in for a rocky landing.
THUD
Oof!
The backs of rovers are not known for their plushness.
It beats landing in the lava.

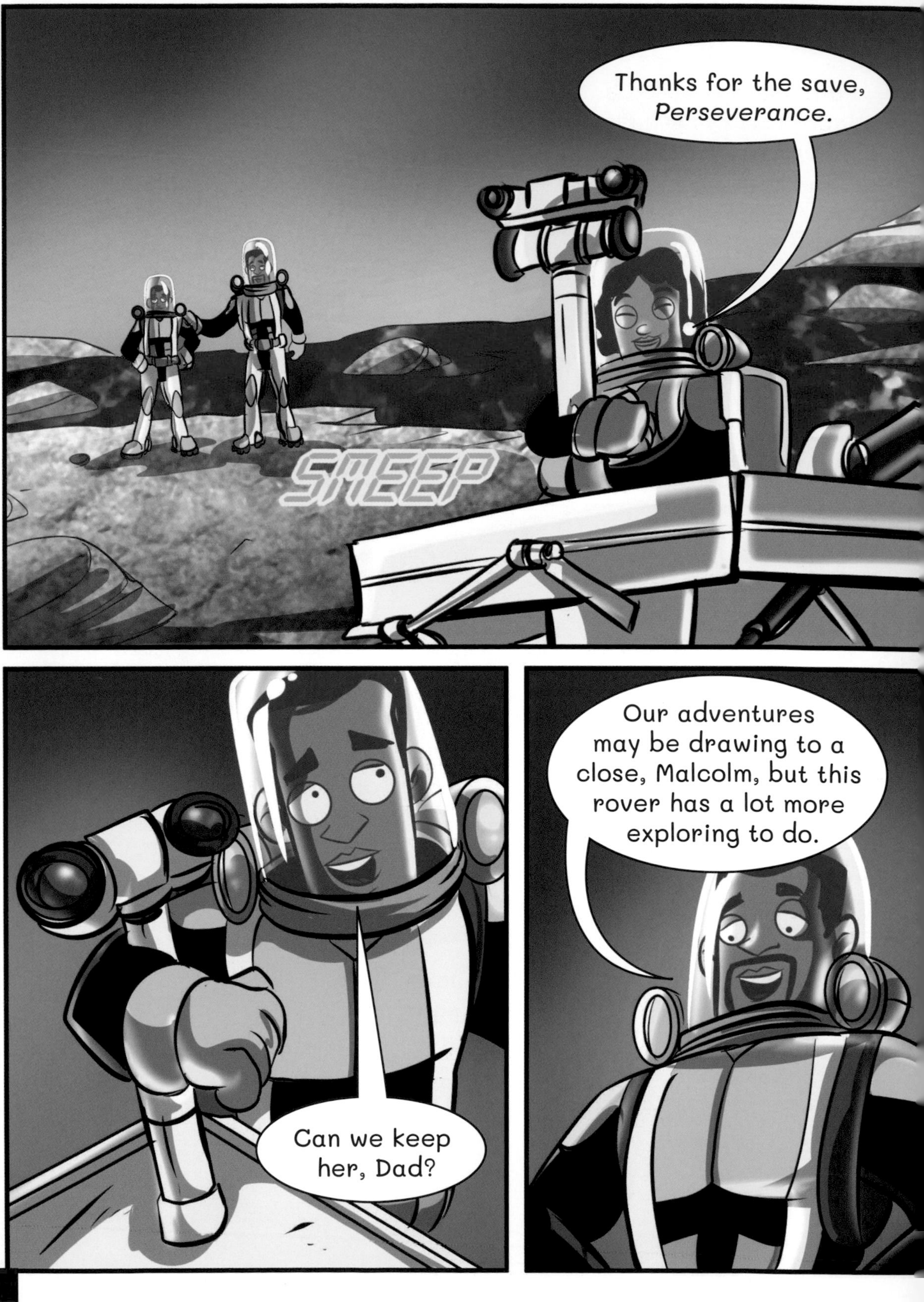
Thanks for the save, *Perseverance.*
SWEEP
Can we keep her, Dad?
Our adventures may be drawing to a close, Malcolm, but this rover has a lot more exploring to do.

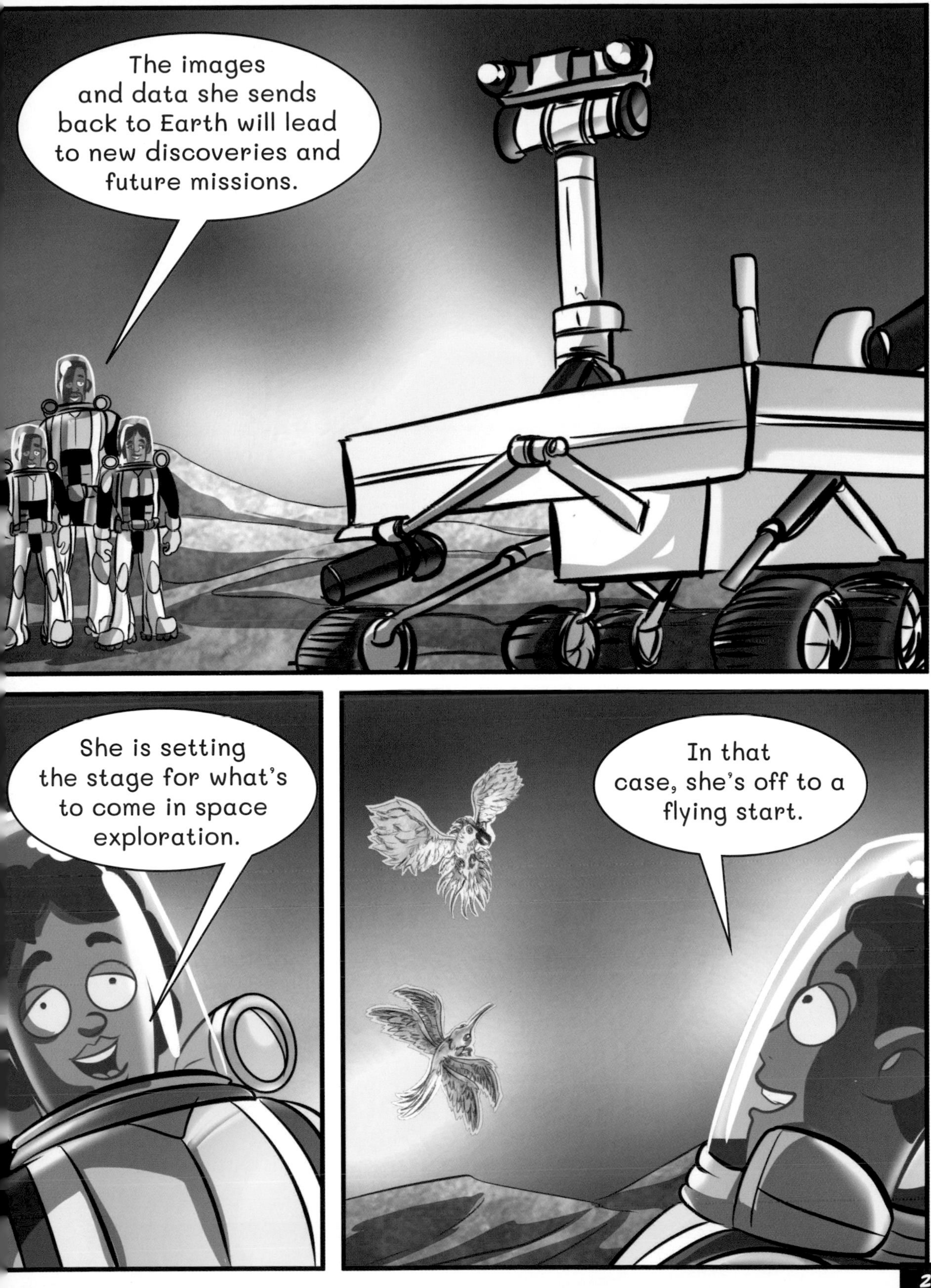
The images and data she sends back to Earth will lead to new discoveries and future missions.
She is setting the stage for what's to come in space exploration.
In that case, she's off to a flying start.

GROOVY LAVA

Lava may be flowing on Mars, but did you know that you can create your own lava lamp at home using a few common household items?

WHAT YOU NEED

- clear bottle
- vegetable oil
- water
- food coloring
- effervescent tablet (antacid medication)

STEPS TO TAKE

1. Fill the bottle almost to the top with vegetable oil.

2. Add a few splashes of water. The water will sink to the bottom.

3. Add a few drops of food coloring to the mixture. This will also sink the bottom.

4. Break the effervescent tablet up into smaller pieces. Drop them in the oil. What happens to the food coloring?

5. To repeat the eruptions, simply add more pieces of the effervescent tablet.

SAFETY PAUSE

Medicine is not a toy. Use only under adult supervision.

LEARN MORE

BOOKS

Bolte, Mari. *Earth vs. Mars*. Ann Arbor, MI: Cherry Lake Publishing, 2022.

Golusky, Jackie. *Explore Mars*. Minneapolis, MN: Lerner Publications, 2021.

WEBSITES

Mars Volcanoes
https://airandspace.si.edu/exhibitions/exploring-the-planets/online/solar-system/mars/surface/volcanoes

Mars is home to the largest volcano in our solar system. But it's not the only one! Find out about all the volcanoes that helped shape the Red Planet.

NISE Network: Exploring the Solar System: Mars Rovers
https://www.nisenet.org/catalog/exploring-solar-system-mars-rovers

Learn about the rovers that explore Mars, and then take on the challenge of designing your own rover.

THE MARTIANS

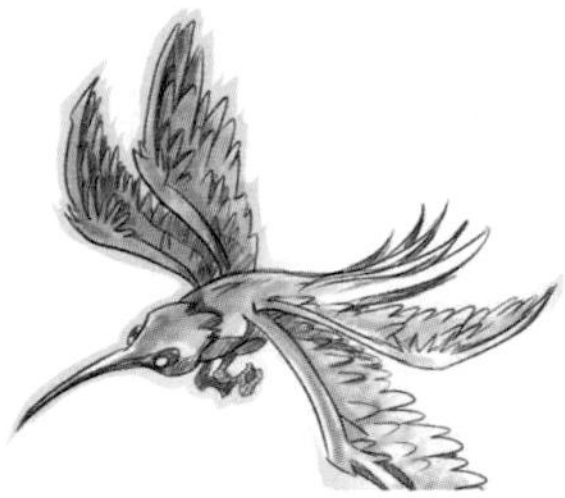

MAGMA ORIOLES

With a beak like a hummingbird, Malcolm imagines this Martian flier sipping from the magma that seeps out from the cracks around the Valles Marineris.

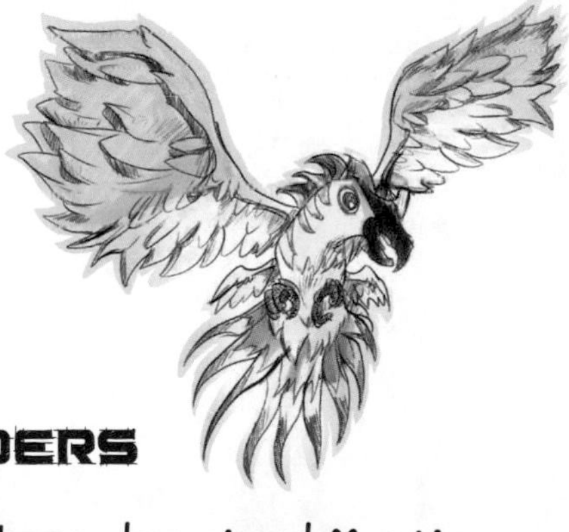

TOUCANYONIERS

Colorful and flamboyant, Malcolm sees this flock-dwelling Martian soaring in and around the Valles Marineris.

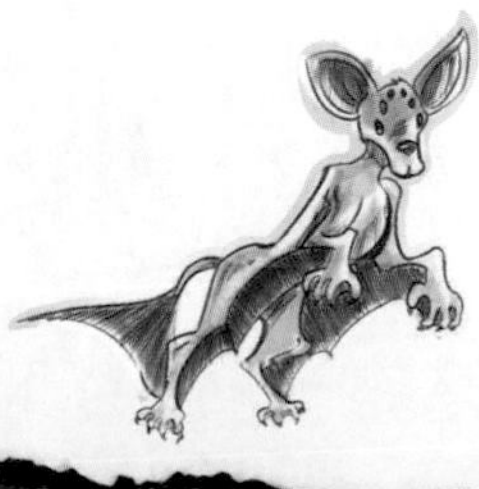

DINGO GLIDERS

Malcolm draws these dog-sized Martians with hands like humans. Malcolm imagines them to be expert hunters that can glide from side to side of the Valles Marineris.

GLOSSARY

buttes (BYOOTS) tall towers of rock with a flat surface

flocks (FLOKS) numbers of birds that feed, rest, or travel together

gravitational pull (grav-uh-TAY-shuh-nuhl PULL) when things with mass or energy are brought toward one another

liquid latex (LIK-wid LAY-tex) a substance that hardens into a rubbery skin

magma (MAYG-muh) liquid rock that is extremely hot

mesas (MEY-suhs) hills or mountains with a flat top

migration (my-GRAY-shuhn) when anima move from one place to another

patagium (peh-TAY-gee-uhm) a thin laye of tissue that helps an animal glide or f

seismic (SIGHS-mik) vibrations in the landscape, both above ground and belo

tide (TIED) the rising and falling of the sea

updraft (UP-draft) a current of air tha travels upward

INDEX